BOTH
PUBLISHING

Published in 2022 by BOTH Publishing.

A CIP catalogue record of this book is available from the British Library

ISBN - 978-1-913603-20-5
eBook available - ISBN - 978-1-913603-21-2

Printed by Ingram Spark.
Distributed by BOTH Publishing.

Cover design and typeset by Chrissey Harrison. Cover illustration by Aphelleon licensed via Shutterstock.

Part of the Dyslexic Friendly Quick Reads Project.

www.booksonthehill.co.uk

SIX LIGHTS OFF GREEN SCAR

Gareth L. Powell

Other dyslexic friendly quick read titles from BOTH publishing

Blood Toll

Silver for Silence

Sharpe's Skirmish

The House on the Old Cliffs

Ultrasound Shadow

The Clockwork Eyeball

Anchor Point

At Midnight I Will Steal Your Soul

Sherlock Holmes and the
Four Kings of Sweden

The Man Who Would Be King

Foreword

By Peter James

Back in 2010 I wrote my first *Quick Reads* novella, *THE PERFECT MURDER*. This was written as adult fiction but with no long words, and was aimed at people who struggled in some way with literacy.

I was lucky enough to win the *Reader's Favourite Award*. At the reception, I was approached by a lady in her late 50s who was close to tears. She told me my novella was the first book she had ever read that was not written for children.

For years she had been too embarrassed ever to read in public – on a beach, a park or a bus or a train – because the only stories she was able to cope with were children's books.

Looking at the dyslexic friendly books BOTH published last year I can see how the larger spacing between the words and larger print create an easy-to-read and accessible format without detracting from the narrative journey. I am excited to be part of their project as it is thanks to initiatives such as the work BOTH is doing, that the condition of dyslexia is now catered for in fiction, and people, such as the lady I met, can hold her head up and read in public, like so many other ordinary people.

Six

Lights

off

Green

Scar

1

NOW

Roulette ships were dangerous and sexy.
They were small and fast and tough.
Their hulls were black tungsten alloy laced
with smart carbon filament. They looked a
bit like flint arrowheads. The media called
them "roulette" ships because they were
used for random jumping.

Random jumping was an extreme
sport. It was the ultimate gamble. It was
a pilot throwing his craft into hyperspace
on a random trajectory, just to see where
he'd end up.

Some discovered habitable planets,

or rich mineral deposits. They became celebrities. They brought back wild tales of bizarre planetary systems, of swollen stars and uncharted asteroid belts.

But the risks were huge. Roulette pilots gambled with their lives, and there were ugly rumours of ghost ships, of murder and cannibalism, and individuals dying lonely, lingering deaths in distant star systems.

Those lucky enough to find their way home clustered on worlds close to the edge of familiar space, where they could stand under the clear night sky and see the unexplored frontier stretching away before them. Pik Station was one such world. It was a dirty little outpost on a half-forgotten moon. Its buildings were low and squalid, like bunkers. Down by the spaceport, drifters and tired hustlers worked its narrow streets. They huddled at its windy intersections in flapping coats, waiting for the right deal, the big score.

Sal Dervish moved among them, avoiding the ebb and flow of their skinny bodies. He wore a heavy coat and a set of stained ship fatigues. His breath came in ragged clouds and his insulated boots crunched solidly on the icy ground. He was the master of the *Wild Cat*, an old roulette ship in storage at the port. She needed an overhaul but he couldn't afford it. Some days, he could hardly afford to eat.

The bar he was heading for was a squat, scrappy affair, built of packing crates and corrugated iron. Whenever a shuttle lifted from the port, its walls and windows shook. As he opened the door, a woman detached herself from the counter and came over.

"Captain Dervish?" She had a reedy accent and wore a smart green parka with the hood thrown back.

He squinted. "Are you Vance?"

She took his elbow and guided him to a table near the fireplace, where two glasses and a bottle of local rot had been laid out.

"Call me Tamara," she said. She poured the drinks and handed him one. As he sipped it, he studied her. She had hair the colour of copper, pulled back into a loose ponytail. When she spoke, it was from the side of her mouth.

"Thank you for coming," she said, "I know it can't have been easy."

Sal put down his glass. "How do you want to do this?"

She looked at him from beneath her long lashes.

"Take a seat," she said.

When they were settled, she activated her voice recorder and leant across the filmy table.

She said, "Let's start at the beginning."

"The beginning?" Sal scratched his nose...

They were trolling around a brown dwarf six lights off Green Scar when they found the derelict ship.

"It looked like hell," he said. "Like something from a sewer."

Tamara nodded. She had her attention focused on the recorder, adjusting the sound levels.

"And this was a random jump?"

He took the bottle and refilled his glass.

"It was our fourth jump in a row," he said. "We were going for the record."

"So what happened?"

"What happened?" He puffed his cheeks out; even now, he could feel the adrenalin tingling in his blood, the breath catching in his throat.

He said, "We found a derelict ship,

like nothing we'd ever seen. Kate said it would be worth a fortune."

Tamara consulted her notebook. "She was the first aboard?"

He nodded. "She went over with Petrov. They wanted to take some pictures, collect some samples, that sort of thing."

"And something attacked them?"

He pushed back on his stool. "They started screaming," he said. "There was something in there, taking them apart."

"And so you turned tail and ran?" Tamara said.

He clenched his fists. "They were already dying," he said. "There was something in there with them, something horrible."

He wiped a hand across his forehead.

"Are you okay?" she asked.

He took a deep breath. He said, "I don't like talking about it."

She looked him in the eye, her gaze long and cool, like the snow outside. She said, "I'm paying you."

He shifted uncomfortably.

She said, "I've heard the stories. I know the other pilots treat you as a pariah, a jinx. They say you've lost your nerve and you'll never jump again." She reached over and touched his wrist. Her fingertips were cold and rough, like frost. "But you used to be a big star, back in the day. People want to find out what happened to you, how you ended up in this desolate wasteland." She waved her hand in a gesture that encompassed the bar, the street, and the dirty snowfields beyond.

He turned away. He wished he'd never agreed to meet her.

"I'm offering you a way out," she said, "a way to redeem yourself."

"I don't care about that."

She withdrew her hand. She put her glass down and pushed it away with her fingernails.

"You cared about Kate, didn't you?" she said.

He dropped his gaze. "More than you'll ever know."

"Then come with me. I'm going in search of your derelict, and I want you to come along. I want to get your reactions, see the thing through your eyes."

She tapped a painted fingernail on the plastic casing of her recorder. "It could be a great story, Sal."

He stood. The legs of his stool scraped loudly on the concrete floor. Around the bar, several heads turned his way.

"I've spent the last two years trying to forget," he said.

She leaned back, arms folded.

"And has it worked?"

THEN

Kate Schnitzler was an engineer. Her hands were rough and she had dirt under her nails. She wore canvas dungarees and a grease-stained t-shirt. She liked machines for their dependability and precision. She had hair the colour of sunlight and she made a point of brushing her teeth every evening, no matter how tired or drunk or lazy she felt. She liked the smell of engine grease and she liked to have her back stroked after sex. When not sharing his cabin, she slept in the cargo bay, curled in an old inflatable life raft from the ship's emergency locker. The orange distress beacon threw eerie moving shadows across the walls.

"When you're running from something, you can't trust a soul," she once said. "Not friends or family – they know who you are, where you go, what you do. To get away, you've got to change, got to do something unexpected."

It took him a month to get up the courage to ask her what she was running from. They were welding a buckled hull plate at the time, in the heat and dust of a dry desert world. She pushed up her black goggles and fixed him with sad eyes.

"We're all running from something, Sal," she said. "People like us don't belong anywhere. Wherever we are, we've always got one eye on the exit, one foot out the door."

She stretched her bare arms over her head. "It's like we were given the wrong lives, you know? Like we've been running from them for so long that we can't remember what it feels like to be still."

It was nearly midday and the hot wind blew thin fans of sand and ash across the runway's shimmering tarmac. She put her arms around his waist and her hair tickled his chin.

"We're like sharks," she said. "We have to keep moving, or we suffocate."

2

NOW

Random jumps through hyperspace were often rough, like passing through white-hot plasma. Only streamlined ships with heavy-duty heat shielding could batter their way through. Ships like the *Wild Cat*, for instance. They were sturdy and dependable. They were designed for abuse. You could slam one into a rocky moon at Mach Four and probably walk away from the wreckage unscathed. Even so, Tamara Vance knew that most professional "roulette" pilots wound up dead sooner or later. They just kept pushing the envelope, racking up the odds until something broke. It didn't matter how safe their ships were, or how tough; the danger was addictive, compelling. These guys just kept tempting fate until something gave.

Take Sal, for instance.

As a roulette pilot, he'd seen strange and terrible things, and staked his claim on half a dozen new worlds. He'd jumped deeper into the unknown than anyone else. Where other pilots crumbled or collapsed, where they lost their nerve, he kept flying. He wasn't afraid, and that lack of feeling had given him an edge. For a short time, it had made him unbeatable. It was only when he met Kate that he appeared to let his guard down. For the first time, he became vulnerable. He started worrying about someone else.

Back in her hotel room, Tamara felt jittery, the way she always did when working on a big story. But this time, it was worse than usual. There was something about Sal Dervish that annoyed and fascinated her. He was a wreck, and she wanted to understand why. But more than that, she wanted to help him.

She stripped off and stepped into the shower. She let the warm water drum into the kinks in her shoulders. She told herself she shouldn't get involved, that she should concentrate on the story. She had her career to think about.

Random jumping was still big news back in the cities of the Assembly's comfortable inner systems. For people whose only experience of flight was a twice-daily trip on a commuter shuttle, the idea of people like Sal Dervish hurling themselves into hyperspace was a wild, almost unbearably exciting prospect: it meant they could emerge almost anywhere and find almost anything. Some random jumpers had grown wealthy and famous from their discoveries. It was a good way to get rich quick, and a good way to get killed.

She rubbed shampoo into her hair. In ancient times, she thought, they'd have been shamans. They'd have been the ones dosing themselves on whatever drugs came to hand, pushing the boundaries of reality in search of answers. They'd have been out there, cavorting in the firelight while the rest of the tribe lived their trip vicariously, too scared to take the plunge themselves.

To a reporter like her, it was a goldmine. It was compulsive, must-see entertainment. And she knew she'd been incredibly lucky to track down Sal Dervish. He'd been such a high-profile burnout that no one in the random jumping community seriously expected him to jump again. After two years in the wilderness, he'd become an almost mythical figure, halfway between an urban legend and a cautionary tale.

She stepped out of the shower and pulled on a robe. If she could take him back to the scene of his downfall and make him face his fear, then this time next year, she'd be sitting behind an anchor's desk, where she belonged.

She had all her hopes pinned on this story. Too many to let her relax and wait for his call. She needed to be active. She got dressed and went out, making sure she had her phone in her pocket.

It took her only a little over an hour to walk the entire length of the settlement, and she was glad of her parka. She watched condensation freeze on the giant fuel silos at the port. She read the graffiti on a row of old spherical descent modules. She saw a couple of drunken ice miners beat each other senseless in the bloody snow outside one of the crappier downtown bars.

Eventually, fed-up and alone, she found herself wandering the streets on the edge of town. Overhead, the stars burned fierce and blue. The dirty snow squeaked underfoot. The cold air bit at her nose and ears; it scoured her lungs. To someone used to the bright lights of the inner systems, Pik Station was a bitter, dismal place.

In a dingy bistro off a side street, she stopped to thaw. They had an open fire, and she needed to get the chill out of her bones. She ordered a drink and took it to a table near the hearth. But no sooner had she got comfortable than a thin guy with hard bright eyes approached her.

"Miss Vance, I presume?" he said.

She was taken aback. She was used to being recognised on the streets of the inner systems but not out here, in the sticks. She was surprised anyone knew who she was.

He bowed his head and said, "I thought as much. There aren't that many women walking these streets in hand-stitched Swiss snow boots."

He held out a hand and she took it. He looked halfway familiar but she couldn't place him. Beneath his leather coat, he wore a white suit and leather cowboy boots. She could smell his aftershave.

She said, "Have we met?"

He smiled. He lifted her hand and brushed it with his dry lips. There were thick silver rings on his fingers.

"I suppose it's possible," he said. He shrugged off his coat and beckoned the barkeeper.

"My name's Dieter," he said. "Can I buy you a drink?"

3

When Sal got back to the *Wild Cat*,
Laurel-Ann was waiting for him. He'd been
hoping she might've got bored and left.

"Where've you been, Sal?" she said,
smoothing down her vinyl skirt with pale
fingers. The overhead lights glittered off
her lip-gloss. He pushed past her and
staggered down to his cabin. He showered
and slipped into a polyester robe. There
were still a few bottles of rot in the hold.
He took one to his bunk. When she joined
him, he ignored her. He didn't want her
there, didn't even want to look at her.

"Just leave me alone," he said.

She didn't understand. She was nineteen, with bad skin and bleached hair.

"What's the matter, baby? Have I done something wrong?" Her voice was thin and pleading and he hated the sound of it.

He rolled over and pointed at the hatch.

"Just get lost," he said.

Her face fell. For a moment, he thought he caught a glimpse of something vulnerable behind the make-up and breast implants. Then her lip curled. She sniffed, adjusted her top, and gathered her few belongings together. He closed his eyes and listened to her heels stamp across the deck. At the hatch, she paused.

"Fuck you," she said.

When Sal was young, he was awkward
and fidgety and raw. He grew up in
a town near a failing seaport. It was
shrouded in fog most days, and the port
lights made the sky glow a hellish orange.
When it wasn't foggy, it was raining,
and the corrosive salt air blew in off the
muddy grey mouth of the estuary, cold
and sharp like rusty barbed wire.

Lowell Creek, like Pik Station, was the
sort of dismal hinterland most people only
passed through, on their way somewhere
else. Those that stopped and stayed
tended to be lost or desperate, or beyond
caring. Either they were looking for
trouble, or they were trying to hide from
it.

He grew up in a house by the river shore, in a row of fishermen's cottages. At high tide, the lamp light from the front room window spilled out over the muddy creek water. When it rained, the lights of the houses on the far shore swam and smeared. He'd wait there, by that window, when his father was out, waiting for the lights of his little boat to appear through the gloom, listening to the pop and sizzle of the ship-to-shore radio.

Until one night, his father failed to return.

It was the night the *Endurance* exploded. Lightning crackled through the overcast sky. Thunder growled. The waves crashed over the flood defences, smashing their spray against the shingle walls of the house. During lulls, he could hear foghorns out in the channel.

His mother joined him at the window.

"It's time you were off to bed," she said half-heartedly.

He rubbed the glass where it was misting. He could see she didn't mean it, that she wanted his company.

"Just a few minutes more," he said.

Down by the creek, he could see lights: There were kids on the *Endurance*.

She was a rusty old hovercraft, built to transport cargo. She lay in the mud at the back of the creek and the local teenagers used her as a hangout. They sat in her hold, drinking and smoking.

When her leaky fuel tank exploded, the blast shook the windows of his house.

It echoed along the street. Front doors were thrown open and people appeared, pulling coats over their pyjamas. His mother went with them.

It took most of the night to bring the blaze under control. There were kids trapped by the fire. Driving rain and intense heat hampered the rescuers. And all the while, out at sea, Sal's father was drowning. The storm had swamped his small boat. With everyone crowded around the burning *Endurance*, there was no one to hear his final, desperate calls. No one except Sal, listening to the radio as he clung helplessly to the window, too scared to move.

When he was fifteen, he ran away from the pain. He locked his past away, where it couldn't hurt him. He rode the freighters that dragged from world to world. He stowed away. He got his first taste of hyperspace travel. He got a tattoo. He lost his virginity behind a greasy café on a cold world whose name he could never remember.

On Strauli, he was caught on the ground during a hurricane that lasted a year; and on Djatt, he spent three days wandering alone in an arctic blizzard. And yet, there was never anything to match the night the *Endurance* went up. There was nothing that could compare to the fear and helplessness of listening to his father die, alone. And so he became a roulette pilot because nothing could frighten him, nothing could shake him. Nothing… until he heard Kate scream. It brought back the awful, freezing dread of that distant rainy night. Alone in the Star Chamber of the *Wild Cat*, he'd been terrified. He'd been a boy again, lost and helpless.

And so he'd fled once more. And he hadn't stopped running until he met Tamara.

THEN

They were seated around the table in the Wild Cat's galley, playing poker.

Kate said, "It's my brother."

"What about him?" Sal thumbed through the cards in his hand. He had six suns and a diamond.

"That's who I'm running from." She tossed a couple of chips into the centre of the table. Beside her, Petrov studied his own cards and frowned.

"It's not my night, I think." He reached for the rot bottle and refilled his glass. Sal ignored him.

"Your brother?"

"My twin brother."

Kate pushed a hand back through her hair and dropped her cards. "I fold."

"Me too." Sal took the bottle from Petrov and made sure her glass was full.

"So, what did he do?"

"My brother?" She shrugged. "It's not so much what he did, as what he does."

"And that is what?" Petrov asked, sweeping his winnings into his lap.

Kate looked away.

"He hurts people," she said.

NOW

Sal woke with a shout. It was past midnight; the lights on the *Wild Cat* were deep brown and his pulse raced. He felt sick.

He slid down to the end of the bunk and opened his footlocker. Near the bottom, among the books and papers, he found his only picture of her. He pulled it out with trembling hands, smoothing down the creased edges. It was a printout captured from a security camera. He'd found it in a pile of her stuff. It showed her laughing, her head thrown back, the line of her throat white against the red silk strap of her dress. She held an empty wine glass carelessly in one hand, a bottle in the other. She had confetti in her hair. He sat on the edge of his bunk and held it to his forehead. He rocked back and forth.

One of Laurel-Ann's pink bauble earrings lay on the deck. He kicked it away savagely, feeling ashamed.

Losing Kate had ripped open old wounds, leaving him scared and vulnerable. It had crippled him.

He clenched his fists, crumpling her picture. He could hear her screams in his head. He couldn't stop them, couldn't block them out. He raged around the ship, pounding the bulkheads with his fists, kicking and slapping the doors and consoles until his hands and feet bled.

Panting, he collapsed into the pilot's chair. Kate's picture was torn; there were pieces missing. He caught sight of his reflection in the console screens; he looked old and beaten.

Everything that was wrong in his life, all the guilt and self-loathing, had its root in that one moment of freezing panic when he'd run, abandoning her. And he'd give anything to be able to go back and do things differently.

But how could he?

Should he take up Tamara Vance's

offer? He sat up straight and wiped his eyes. Everything here was so screwed up, what was there to lose? He couldn't go on like this, carrying this burden of grief and remorse. He needed a way to make amends, to atone for his cowardice.

He had to go back to Green Scar and do what he should've done in the first place. And, if he didn't survive, it would make things right, it would be a redemption.

He called Tamara Vance and she answered on the third ring.

He said, "I'm in."

She said, "I'll be right over."

4

Sal glanced across to where Dieter leaned against the landing bay door, just out of earshot.

"I don't trust him," he said.

Tamara rolled her eyes. She was standing on the boarding ramp of the *Wild Cat*. Sal sat at the top. His boots were undone and he was bare-chested. His forearms rested lightly on his knees. He'd been helping the maintenance crew to weld new hull plates in place, in preparation for their flight, and his skin shone with sweat and grease. Tamara's money had allowed him to make his ship spaceworthy again, but he knew the repairs were only temporary fixes. They'd last long enough to do what needed to be done.

"Look at him, look at the way he's dressed. He's a thug," he said in a low voice. "He's a small time gangster wannabe and I don't want him on my ship."

"I really wish you'd reconsider."

Sal ran a hand through his dirty hair. He could smell his own sweat.

"I'm sorry," he said, "but there's no way."

Tamara rocked back on her heels. She said, "Think of him as a rich tourist looking for a thrill."

Sal stood up and wiped his palms

together. "I'm sorry."

Seeing the gesture, Dieter straightened up and stepped forward. He was wearing thin black sunglasses and a wide, floppy hat. His boot heels clicked loudly on the bay's metal floor.

"Mister Dervish," he called, "I have an offer which may change your mind."

Sal turned. He spread his hands. "I really doubt it," he said.

"You haven't heard it yet."

Dieter stopped walking. He took his glasses off and fixed Sal with a steady stare.

"If you'll take me, I'm willing to pay you two hundred thousand," he said.

Sal grunted. "Credits? Or local funny money?"

"Credits."

He whistled. "The whole ship isn't worth that much."

Dieter reached into the pocket of his white coat. He pulled out a bundle of laminated notes and tossed them onto the boarding ramp.

"At a generous estimate, Mister Dervish, your ship's worth a hundred and ninety thousand Credits. You can consider the rest payment for your services."

Sal tried to keep a straight face. He had to admit he was tempted. With that kind of money, he could completely refit the *Wild Cat*, or sell her and retire. He could start a new life, somewhere nobody knew him.

Just thinking about it made him ache

because he wanted it so much.

Tamara put a hand on his shoulder.

"Please?" she said.

An hour later, the *Wild Cat* blasted into the cold dawn sky. Once above the grey clouds, she turned as if questing for a scent. Sal, in the Star Chamber at her heart, watched as navigation solutions popped up around him. Their flashing yellow overlays marked potential destinations within range. He paused, taking in the sweep of possibilities. In the chair beside him, Tamara looked up from her notes.

"Are you ready?" she said.

He nodded, trying to look more

confident that he felt. "As ready as we'll ever be."

The co-ordinates were still in the ship's memory, where they'd lain hidden for the last two years. He took a deep breath and engaged the Bradley engines. His heart hammered in his chest.

Three hours later, they emerged near an unremarkable brown dwarf six lights from the Green Scar system. They were just beyond the rim of explored space, out on the ragged edge of the frontier. The ride through hyperspace had been long and rough, worse than he remembered.

He pulled up a wraparound display of

the system. The brown dwarf was on their starboard side. An insistent red cursor to port showed the position of the alien derelict.

Tamara said, "How close do you think we can get?"

He took a deep breath. He was beginning to have second thoughts. He needed time to nerve himself.

"I don't know."

Behind him, Dieter unfastened his safety restraints and stood up.

"You're going on board," he said.

Sal turned to him. "What?"

"You heard me." Dieter reached into his jacket and pulled out a stubby, business-like pistol.

Sal said, "What the hell are you doing?"

He looked at Tamara. She wouldn't look at him. Her chin dropped onto her chest.

"Dieter is Kate's brother," she said.

Dieter leaned over him. He smelled of aftershave and sweat. When he spoke, a gold canine caught the light.

"You ran out on her," he said.

Sal turned away. "It wasn't like that."

Dieter pointed the gun at him and said, "You left her to die and you ran, to save yourself."

Sal looked down at the metal deck

and shook his head. He said, "There was nothing I could do. I wish there was."

Dieter took a step back. He indicated the red cursor on the display. He said, "You're going to go over there and bring back her body."

Tamara said, "That's suicide."

Dieter ignored her. He leaned in close again. His skin was the colour of sand and his breath made Sal's nose wrinkle.

"You owe her that much," Dieter said.

Sal turned his face away. "You know she spent her life running from you, don't you?" he said.

Dieter scowled. "She was my sister. You lost her, and I want her back."

He straightened up. He held the gun in front of him. "I want her back, and you're going to get her for me."

Sal clenched his fists.

"I'm not doing anything for you," he
said.

Dieter's lip curled. His pistol swung
toward Tamara. Sal saw what was about
to happen and shouted: "Leave her
alone!"

Tamara squirmed in her seat, tried to
turn away, but the safety harness held
her in place.

She yelped as Dieter shot her.

"Sal?" she said. "Sal?"

She pressed her hands over the wound
in her thigh, trying to staunch the flow

of blood. It welled up thickly between her fingers. Sal popped his straps and grabbed an emergency patch from the medkit. He pushed her hands away slapped it over the ragged hole in her sodden fatigues.

He rounded on Dieter. He yelled: "Why the hell did you do that?"

Dieter looked down at him. "That patch will stop the bleeding," he said, "but it can't repair an artery. If you don't get her to a hospital in the next few hours, she'll lose that leg. Maybe even die.'

Sal looked at the blood on his hands. He felt angry and helpless. He looked at Tamara.

She said, "It hurts."

Dieter aimed the gun at her other leg. With his free hand, he reached over and took Sal by the shoulder. He pushed him towards the pilot's chair.

"If you want to save her, you'll have to find Kate," he said.

Sal strapped himself in. He didn't have any choice. His hands were shaking as he reached out and grasped the controls.

"Hold on," he said.

He brought them in fast, but the black ship was waiting. It attacked as soon as they were close enough. Shards burst from it like porcupine quills and punched into their hull. They felt the impacts through the floor.

"What was that?" Tamara asked, with her eyes closed.

Damage reports clamoured for Sal's attention. He pulled up a summary. "Multiple kinetic hits, like a shotgun blast," he said. "We've lost the cameras on the port side and we're leaking air."

Behind him, Dieter held the back of his couch. Tamara looked sick.

"Can you bring us around, get the starboard cameras on the derelict?" she said.

"I'll try."

On the tactical display, the black ship was a shadow moving against the stars; he had to infer its shape from memory. Off to one side, the star known as Green

Scar burned against the pale wash of the Milky Way.

The derelict fired a second volley. The *Wild Cat* shuddered as it hit and the lights in the Star Chamber flickered.

"I just keep thinking too much," Sal said.

He felt the gun press into the back of his neck. Dieter said, "What?"

Sal pictured Kate and Laurel-Ann. He felt the weight of the last two years, pressing down on him.

"I just want it to stop," he said.

He aimed the *Wild Cat*'s nose at the alien ship and threw open the throttle.

There are two kinds of courage. There's the kind you get from knowing that what you're doing is right. And there's the kind you get from knowing it's hopeless and wrong, and just not giving a damn.

In the seconds before the impact, his fear vanished. He was ready to go out in a blaze of glory if it meant wiping the slate clean. He let out a loud laugh: This was how it used to be on a random jump, how it used to feel. He was totally connected to the moment. Adrenalin hammered in his veins. Everything felt fierce and primal and inevitable. And it all moved so damn fast.

He'd almost forgotten how good it felt...

For half a second, in the roar of the exhaust, he thought he heard Kate calling to him. Only this time, it wasn't fear in her voice, it was forgiveness.

THEN

"Nothing in the main corridor," Petrov reported.

Sal didn't bother to reply; his attention was taken up with the thermal imaging scan, which produced a ghostly image of the two figures in the narrow corridor.

"Nothing but this crap," Kate said, eyeing the slimy, dripping walls with distaste.

She moved like a dancer, lightly on the balls of her feet. The slug thrower in her right hand wavered back and forth with the sweep of her gaze.

"Are you picking up any signs of life?" she said.

Sal could feel the tension in his back and forearms; his fists were clenching and unclenching. He tried to relax, but he'd heard the stories, same as everyone else.

"There's nothing on the monitors," he said.

"I hear you, my friend." Petrov was already chipping away at the walls with a chisel.

"Hey, careful," Kate said. She sounded so close that it was easy to forget she was three kilometres away, in the belly of a strange and potentially dangerous alien derelict.

"I love you," he said, into the microphone.

5

The *Wild Cat* crashed against the hideous black ship and the impact cracked her tough hull. Her spine buckled; her heat shield tore apart, and she fell from the larger vessel like a bug falling from a windshield.

In the spherical Star Chamber at her heart, the virtual screens flared and died; part of the ceiling collapsed; sparks flew from crippled instrument panels and burning plastic fumes filled the air.

Sal Dervish sagged against the crash webbing in his couch. His neck hurt. With most of the external cameras gone, he was blind and disorientated; unable to tell where he was, or what state his ship was in. His only functioning screens showed empty space, distant stars.

He looked around for Dieter. Without straps to restrain him, the young man had been catapulted forward and smashed against an instrument panel. There was blood in his hair and his head lay at an awkward angle.

In the co-pilot's position, Tamara Vance lolled against her straps, unconscious. They were here because of her. Her eyes were closed, her face slack. He reached out to touch her hand and she started.

"What happened?" she said. There was blood on her chin, where she'd bitten her lip. "Did we kill it?"

Sal shook his head. "We hit it, but I don't think it noticed. It slapped us aside and kept right on going."

"And we survived?" She sounded unsure. She rubbed her forehead with the back of her hand.

He nodded. He ran his fingertips over the unresponsive instruments. His pulse was racing, hammering in his ears. There was a bubbling laugh in his throat and he had to bite down hard, afraid to let it out.

"I told you this ship was tough," he said. "How's the leg?"

"Painful." She dabbed tentatively at the blood on her chin with the sleeve of her flight suit. Her ponytail was coming loose and untidy strands of copper-coloured hair fell around her face. Sal gave her a grin. He could see she was shaken but he couldn't help it. A burden had been lifted from him. He'd done penance for his cowardice, thrown himself into battle and emerged alive, if not triumphant.

"Did you get it all on film?" he asked.

The corner of her mouth twitched upward. She still held the recorder in her lap, although the cables connecting it to the ship's systems had been ripped loose.

"Everything up until the crash," she said.

He unbuckled and reached for Dieter's gun. He picked it up and blew dust off the barrel. It was a matt black plastic pistol. It looked ugly and vicious and expensive, and it felt great.

"What are you going to do with that?" she said.

"I don't know." he said, shrugging. He just wanted to hold it. It was a victory celebration, like a finger of defiance to the universe that had – once again – failed to kill him.

He pointed it at Dieter. "Why didn't you tell me who he was?" he said.

"Because I knew you'd never let him on board, and getting both of your reactions was too good an opportunity to pass up," Tamara said.

She swivelled around and tapped the instrument panel with distaste. The few functioning readouts showed only that the Bradley engines were offline and haemorrhaging fuel.

"So, how do we get home? We're still venting oxygen and it looks to me like the ship's pretty wrecked."

He knew he should be angry with her for lying to him, but he couldn't summon up the energy. Instead, he closed one eye and sighted the gun on Dieter's forehead. He pictured himself pulling the trigger.

"We've got an automatic distress beacon," he said.

"No-one's going to hear that before we run out of air. We're in the middle of nowhere."

He closed his eyes. His euphoria was gone and all he really wanted now was to go back to his cabin, grab a shower and get some sleep.

"The chances are slim," he admitted.

"Then what do you suggest?" she said through gritted teeth.

He scanned the room. There was an emergency locker marked with red flashes. He pulled it open and brought out a couple of lightweight pressure suits.

"We'll use these," he said. "Their air recyclers are good for days. We'll have time to think of something."

She looked down. "What about Dieter?" she said.

Sal grunted and put a hand on the back of his neck, where it still hurt. "Let's stuff him in one of the emergency sleep tanks and worry what to do with him later."

They were quiet for a moment, unwilling to look at each other. They both knew that with his injuries, there was a good chance Dieter wouldn't survive the freezing process.

Eventually, Tamara pulled herself upright and looked down at her bloody thigh. She smoothed back her hair and folded her arms.

"Screw him," she said.

Over the next few hours, the *Wild Cat* faded around them like a candle guttering. Sal didn't think she'd ever fly properly again; her back was broken, her engines wrecked. Despite the efforts of her auto-repair packages, her vital systems were failing one by one, leaking away or freezing in the darkness.

He sat there, in his control couch, with the black box resting on his knees and Dieter's pistol in a thigh pocket. The air in his suit smelled of sweat and fear. The overhead lights sparked and fluttered fitfully as the power fluctuated in the damaged reactor. And all the while, he thought of Kate.

"Tell me about her," Tamara said, in one of her lucid moments.

Sal wrinkled his nose; he didn't want to talk about her, not now, at the end.

He said, "She was just the most incredible person I ever met."

He hugged himself as best he could in the cumbersome suit. The temperature on the bridge had been falling steadily and was already well below freezing.

He began to feel light-headed and drowsy. Despite what he'd told Tamara, the air recyclers weren't designed for long duration use and probably wouldn't last much longer, certainly no more than a day.

She coughed and muttered. The painkillers had worn off and she was slipping in and out of a tormented sleep. Beneath her visor, she looked weak and pale.

"This wasn't how it was supposed to be," Sal said, aware he was talking to himself. A long, drawn-out death wasn't something he'd bargained for when he decided to ram the alien ship. He'd hoped to go out in a blaze of glory and redemption, not linger here, slowly fading. His empty stomach was an uncomfortable knot. His throat was dry. His suit itched and chafed. But somehow, none of it really mattered. What mattered was that he'd come here to make peace with the past. He'd made a decision and faced the consequences. His only regret was that Tamara had to share his fate. But then, without her cajoling, he might never have come back. He might have died alone, on Pik Station, in disgrace.

He used the functioning console to divert the last of the ship's power to the self-repair packages, hoping it might buy them a bit more time. And then he lay and looked at the ceiling. Beside him, sexless in her thick pressure suit, Tamara groaned and swore and thrashed. She was disorientated from the drugs. She clawed at her faceplate with gloved fingers until he used the medical interface on the wrist of her suit to trigger morphine into her system.

"We're going to die," she sobbed, her cries melting into the warmth of the drug. "We can't last more than a few days without water. We're both going to die."

He did his best to keep her comfortable. He thought about putting her into one of the emergency sleep tanks next to Dieter's, but couldn't summon the energy. As the hours wore away, his eyelids became heavier and heavier. His thoughts became slippery and vague. He saw Kate's face. He saw the dark muddy water of Lowell Creek. And then...

An insistent beeping in his headphones woke him. He stirred, moving stiffly. His lips felt cracked and his fingers and toes hurt because they were so cold.

Beneath a thin layer of frost, there were a handful of lights blinking on the control console. The self-repair packages had brought the Bradley engines back online.

He nudged Tamara. "Hey, we've got power," he said.

But even as he spoke, something caught his eye. On one of the remaining functional screens, something big and black moved purposefully against the stars. A proximity warning pinged on the main flight console as the ship's autopilot tagged the intruder, logging its position and vector as a possible threat.

Tamara opened her eyes. She looked awful. Her head swayed from side-to-side, weighed down by the helmet.

"We can go home?" she said.

Sal bit his lip. They could jump into hyperspace, but the heat shielding was damaged and they had no way to navigate.

"The black ship's coming back," he said.

He glanced over, but she'd closed her eyes again. He ran a quick check on her air supply and frowned at the result. She was good for a couple of hours, maybe. She had enough oxygen to make it back to Pik Station, if he could take them straight there. But he had no way to navigate. They could end up anywhere, if they didn't burn up in the process.

He felt his lips twitch in a smile.

"No air and a damaged heat shield," he said. Surely this would be the ultimate random jump – if they survived it, he'd get his reputation back, whether he wanted it or not.

He looked at the screen: The black ship was closing. It would be in striking range in six seconds.

Four seconds.

He reached out and placed his gauntleted hand on the touch screen that controlled the Bradley engines. Despite the cold, his palms were sweating.

Two seconds.

One.

His lips peeled back in a fierce grin. He pressed down on the screen and the *Wild Cat* groaned. She shook herself like a wounded animal, and leapt.

About the Author

Gareth L. Powell writes science fiction about extraordinary characters wrestling with the question of what it means to be human. He has won and been shortlisted for several major awards and his *Embers of War* novels are currently being adapted for TV.

You can find out more at: www.garethlpowell.com

Also by Gareth L. Powell

The Continuance Series

Stars and Bones

The Embers of War Series

Embers of War
Fleet of Knives
Light of Impossible Stars

The Ack-Ack Macaque Series

Ack-Ack Macaque
Hive Monkey
Macaque Attack

Standalone Novels

The Recollection
Silversands

More dyslexic friendly

titles coming soon...

BOTH
PUBLISHING